A Note to Parents

DK READERS is a compelling program for beginning readers, designed in conjunction with leading literacy experts, including Dr. Linda Gambrell, Director of the Eugene T. Moore School of Education at Clemson University. Dr. Gambrell has served on the Board of Directors of the International Reading Association and as President of the National Reading Conference.

Beautiful illustrations and superb full-color photographs combine with engaging, easy-to-read stories to offer a fresh approach to each subject in the series. Each DK READER is guaranteed to capture a child's interest while developing his or her reading skills, general knowledge, and love of reading.

The five levels of DK READERS are aimed at different reading abilities, enabling you to choose the books that are exactly right for your child:

Pre-level 1: Learning to read
Level 1: Beginning to read
Level 2: Beginning to read alone
Level 3: Reading alone
Level 4: Proficient readers

The "normal" age at which a child begins to read can be anywhere from three to eight years old, so these levels are only a general guideline.

No matter which level you select, you can be sure that you are helping your child learn to read, then read to learn!

LONDON, NEW YORK, MUNICH,
MELBOURNE, and DEHLI

Series Editors Deborah Lock, Penny Smith
Art Editor Jacqueline Gooden
U.S. Editors Elizabeth Hester, John Searcy
Production Alison Lenane
DTP Designer Almudena Díaz
Jacket Designer Hedi Gutt

Reading Consultant
Linda Gambrell, Ph.D.

First American Edition, 2005
05 06 07 08 09 10 9 8 7 6 5 4 3 2 1
Published in the United States by DK Publishing, Inc.
375 Hudson Street, New York, New York 10014

DK books are available at special discounts for bulk purchases for sales promotions,
premiums, fundraising, or educational use. For details, contact:
DK Publishing Special Markets
375 Hudson Street
New York, NY 10014
SpecialSales @dk.com

Published in Great Britain by Dorling Kindersley Limited.

A catalog record for this book is available
from the Library of Congress

ISBN 0-7566-1464-3 (Paperback) 0-7566-1463-5 (Hardcover)

Color reproduction by Colourscan, Singapore
Printed and bound in China by L Rex Printing Co., Ltd.

The publisher would like to thank the following for their kind permission
to reproduce their photographs:
a=above; c=center; b=below; l=left; r=right; t=top

Alamy Images: Comstock Images 22-23; Bruce Coleman Inc 27t; BSH Stock 14t;
Colin Harris/ LightTouch Images 8bl; FLPA 16bl; gopi 9bcr; Greg Philpott 9bc; Ian Miles/
Flashpoint Pictures 9bl; Ivor Toms 9br; Lynne Siler/ Focus Group 8br; Mark Sykes 8bcr,
32tc; Robography 9bcl; Stock Connection Distribution 15b. **Corbis:** Ariel Skelley 11, 20b;
Geoff Moon; Frank Lane Picture Agency 17bcl, 17t; Kevin Fleming 6t; Kevin Schafer
17bl, 17br, 32cra; Najlah Feanny 28-29; Norbert Schaefer 26c; Scott T. Smith 17bcr;
Tom Stewart 30-31. **DK Images:** Philip Dowell 29bc. **Getty Images:** Andy Sacks 12-13;
Peter Cade 24-25; Robert Daly 18-19; Yellow Dog Productions 8-9. **N.H.P.A.:** Ernie Janes
16br. **Zefa Visual Media:** Masterfile./ Kevin Dodge 4-5; Noel Hendrickson 16t.

All other images © Dorling Kindersley
For more information see: www.dkimages.com

Discover more at

www.dk.com

DK READERS

LEARNING
TO READ
pre-level 1

Petting Zoo

DK Publishing, Inc.

What kind of animal

We are at the
petting zoo.

do you see here?

We are petting
a drowsy donkey.

 donkeys

ear

hoof

We are walking two baby llamas.

llamas

leash

I am brushing a pony's coat.

mane

  ponies

pigs

I am picking up
a little pink pig.

snout

hoof

hen

 chicks

I am carrying
a soft yellow chick.

chick

 stick insects

leaf

stick insect

I am holding
a green stick insect.

frogs

I am watching
a beady-eyed frog.

Ribbit! Ribbit!

toe

It is mealtime now.
I give the woolly lamb
some milk.

lambs

wool

21

I am feeding
a hungry rabbit.

ear

carrot

rabbits

This fluffy guinea pig
is nibbling a leaf.

 guinea pigs

whiskers

claws

The white goose wants a snack.

 geese

gosling

bill

feathers

 goats

This long-horned goat is eating his lunch.

horn

Goodbye, animals!

It's time to go home.

Picture word list

donkey

page 6

llama

page 8

pony

page 10

pig

page 12

chick

page 14

stick insect

page 16

frog

page 18

lamb

page 20

rabbit

page 22

guinea pig

page 24

goose

page 26

goat

page 28